YASMIN

The Recycler

written by
SAADIA FARUQI

illustrated by
HATEM ALY

PICTURE WINDOW BOOKS
a capstone imprint

To Mariam for inspiring me, and Mubashir
for helping me find the right words—S.F.

To my sister, Eman, and her amazing girls,
Jana and Kenzi—H.A.

Yasmin is published by Picture Window Books, an imprint of Capstone.
1710 Roe Crest Drive
North Mankato, Minnesota 56003
www.capstonepub.com

Text copyright © 2021 by Saadia Faruqi.
Illustrations copyright © 2021 by Capstone.

All rights reserved. No part of this publication may be reproduced
in whole or in part, or stored in a retrieval system, or transmitted in
any form or by any means, electronic, mechanical, photocopying,
recording, or otherwise, without written permission of the publisher.

Library of Congress Cataloging-in-Publication Data is available on the
Library of Congress website.
Names: Faruqi, Saadia, author. | Aly, Hatem, illustrator. Title: Yasmin
the recycler / written by Saadia Faruqi ; illustrated by Hatem Aly.
Description: North Mankato, Minnesota : Picture Window Books,
[2021] | Series: Yasmin | Audience: Ages 5-7. | Audience: Grades K-1. |
Summary: Yasmin is thrilled about her school's new recycling program,
but getting her friends to pitch in is no easy task. Identifiers: LCCN
2020039011 (print) | LCCN 2020039012 (ebook) | ISBN 9781515882619
(hardcover) | ISBN 9781515883746 (paperback) | ISBN 9781515892502
(pdf) | ISBN 9781515893264 (kindle edition) Subjects: CYAC: Recycling
(Waste)—Fiction. | Schools—Fiction. | Pakistani Americans—Fiction.
| Muslims—United States—Fiction. Classification: LCC PZ7.1.F373
Yim 2021 (print) | LCC PZ7.1.F373 (ebook) | DDC [E]—dc23 LC record
available at https://lccn.loc.gov/2020039011 LC ebook record available
at https://lccn.loc.gov/2020039012

Editorial Credits:
Editor: Kristen Mohn; Designer: Kay Fraser; Production Specialist: Tori
Abraham

Design Elements:
Shutterstock: LiukasArt

TABLE OF CONTENTS

Something New at School

One Monday, Principal Nguyen held an assembly. "Our school is starting a new recycling program!" he announced.

"I hope that doesn't mean more homework," Ali whispered.

"Shh," Yasmin whispered back.

Principal Nguyen explained. "Factories can make new things out of old things we no longer need. That is recycling. It's one way to help clean up our planet."

He showed the students a symbol.

"This symbol means an item can be recycled. Starting tomorrow, the whole school will collect plastic and metal items for recycling."

"Hooray!" Yasmin said. "I want to help make the planet clean!"

"I just want lunch!" said Ali.

Emma yawned.

CHAPTER 2

A Difficult Job

The next day, there were big
green bins around the school.

"We're going to be the best
recyclers!" Yasmin said at lunch.

Emma peered into Yasmin's
lunch box.

"You brought parathas! Can I have one?" Emma asked.

"Of course!" Yasmin said.

"Can I try one?" Ali asked.

Yasmin handed him a piece of hers.

Ali took a big bite. "That's delicious! I would do anything for more of those!" he said.

Ali finished his lunch and headed for the bins.

"Don't forget to recycle!"

Yasmin said.

"Oh yeah," Ali said. He tossed

his water bottle toward the bins.

"Two points!" he yelled.

But the bottle landed in the

blue garbage bin, *not* the green

recycling bin.

"No points!" Yasmin called

after him. But Ali didn't hear her.

Principal Nguyen appeared.

"I need some helpers to sort the recycling," he said.

Yasmin stood up. "We'll help!"

Emma shook her head. "Sorry. I have to finish my math."

"But the planet . . . ," Yasmin mumbled.

Didn't her friends want to help?

Yasmin stayed to help the principal. She was sad to see that many kids hadn't put things in the right bins. Plastic items were in the trash. Trash was in the recycling. It was a big mess!

The principal sighed. "The students need encouragement to recycle more. Maybe a party for the class that recycles the most?"

Yasmin thought about her friends at lunch. She smiled. "How about a *paratha* party? I could ask my mama to help!"

"Delicious idea, Yasmin!" Principal Nguyen said. "Let's go call her together."

CHAPTER 3

A Delicious Prize

Yasmin's mama agreed to make parathas for the party. Yasmin couldn't wait to tell her friends during free time!

"Let's make posters to let everyone know," suggested their teacher, Ms. Alex.

"I'll help!" Emma said.

They got out markers and paper. When they were done, Yasmin asked Ali to help hang the posters.

Ali held one up. "A paratha party?" he said. "Now I *love* recycling!"

Yasmin beamed.

Ms. Alex's students brought recycling all week. Yasmin brought empty soap bottles. Emma brought cans her family had collected.

Ali brought in the biggest bag of all. Cans, jugs, and all kinds of bottles!

"We can recycle them all. I looked for the symbol!" Ali said.

Soon the green bins were full.

On Friday, Principal Nguyen
held another assembly.

"Great job recycling,
students!" he said. "The winner
is . . . Ms. Alex's class!"

Everyone cheered.

That afternoon, Yasmin's
mother and Nani delivered lots
of parathas to Ms. Alex's room
for the party.

"Helping the planet is great!" said Yasmin.

"So are parathas!" Ali said, and he took a big bite.

Think About It, Talk About It

* Does your school have a recycling program? If not, write a letter to your principal asking if you could start one.

* What are some ways you help the environment at home? Some families recycle. Some families compost their food scraps. Some families try to reduce their use of gas and electricity. Make a list of the ways your family could help keep the planet clean.

* Yasmin realized that a prize of her mother's parathas might help her friends recycle more. Why was it important that she and Principal Nguyen ask her mother for permission first?

Learn Urdu with Yasmin!

Yasmin's family speaks both English and Urdu. Urdu is a language from Pakistan. Maybe you already know some Urdu words!

baba (BAH-bah)—father

hijab (HEE-jahb)—scarf covering the hair

jaan (jahn)—life; a sweet nickname for a loved one

kitaab (keh-TAB)—book

lassi (LAH-see)—a yogurt drink

nana (NAH-nah)—grandfather on mother's side

nani (NAH-nee)—grandmother on mother's side

paratha (pa-RAH-tha)—buttery flatbread with layers

salaam (sah-LAHM)—hello

shukriya (shuh-KREE-yuh)—thank you

Pakistan Fun Facts

Yasmin and her family are proud of their Pakistani culture. Yasmin loves to share facts about Pakistan!

Islamabad

PAKISTAN

Pakistan is on the continent of Asia, with India on one side and Afghanistan on the other.

The word Pakistan means "land of the pure" in Urdu and Persian.

Many languages are spoken in Pakistan, including Urdu, English, Saraiki, Punjabi, Pashto, Sindhi, and Balochi.

The word paratha means layers of cooked dough. Paratha is often served with butter, pickles, or other toppings.

Pakistan started a program called Clean Green Pakistan in 2018 to help improve the country's environment.

Make a Recycle Monster

SUPPLIES:

- 2 large brown paper bags
- markers
- scissors
- tape

STEPS:

1. Turn one paper bag up upside down. On the front, draw eyes, a nose, and a big open mouth—big enough to fit bottles and cans through.

2. Cut out the mouth so there is an opening in the middle of the bag.

3. Lay down the second bag right side up and write FEED ME! on it.

4. Draw the recycle symbol underneath the words.

5. Place the first bag over the opening of the second and tape the two open sides together.

6. Place your Recycle Monster in your room, kitchen, or classroom, and feed it recycling!

Saadia Faruqi is a Pakistani American writer, interfaith activist, and cultural sensitivity trainer featured in *O Magazine*. She is author of two middle grade novels, *A Place at the Table* and *A Thousand Questions*. She is also editor-in-chief of *Blue Minaret*, an online magazine of poetry, short stories, and art. Besides writing books, she also loves reading, binge-watching her favorite shows, and taking naps. She lives in Houston, Texas, with her husband and children.

About the Illustrator

Hatem Aly is an Egyptian-born illustrator whose work has been published all over the world. He currently lives in beautiful New Brunswick, Canada, with his wife, son, and more pets than people. When he is not dipping cookies in a cup of tea or staring at blank pieces of paper, he is usually drawing, reading, or daydreaming. You can see his art in books that earned multiple starred reviews and positions on the *NYT* Best-Sellers list, such as *The Proudest Blue* (with Ibtihaj Muhammad & S.K. Ali) and *The Inquisitor's Tale* (with Adam Gidwitz), a Newbery Honor winner.

Join Yasmin on all her adventures!

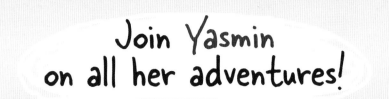